THE Cat WANTS Cuddles

I really don't.

by P. Crumble
Pictures by
Lucinda Gifford

Scholastic Inc.

To AR for loving the cuddliest cat ever — PC

**For Conrad — and the Furphy Bellettes,
who are not afraid to cuddle him — LG**

Library of Congress Cataloging-in-Publication Data available

ISBN 978-1-338-74122-3

10 9 8 7 6 5 4 3 2 1   21 22 23 24 25

Printed in China
This edition first printing, June 2021

The text type was set in Granjon and Noyh A Bistro.

I know! Come on, Kevin,
time for cuddles.

Time for me to go . . .

Kevin?

Keep walking . . .

Let's cuddle!

Don't come
any closer.

Go away, Dog!
Can't you see
I'm hiding?

You're lucky.
No one wants to
cuddle a fish.

There you are, Kevin!
What are you doing
on the shelf?

Trying to get some
peace and quiet!

The Great Catsby

OF MICE AND MEN

PURRFUME

MIAOW'S LAST DANCER

CAT-22

THE THREE MOUSKETEERS

PAWS and PEACE

I mean look at the dog. Does he look like he is enjoying himself?

quite . . .

comfortable.